thanks for
your support
Greg Crowley
12-9-23

0

NOT WORTHY STORY OF REVENGE

Jay Crowley

Join me on Facebook: Jay Crowley-Sweet Dreams Books
For updates on new stories and more information on the author or books, please follow me on Amazon or visit www.sweetdreamsbooks.com

If you have read and enjoyed any of my books -- would you please take the time to go to Amazon or Barnes and Noble, right now and leave a review on the book or books you have read. It would mean so much to me. Thank yo

ALSO BY JAY CROWLEY

Opal

Cabin in the Meadow

Ship in the Desert

A Selection of My Short Stories

Laura

Natalie's Adventures-Middle Grade

A Gift from Nate-Double Lung
Transplant

ANTHOLOGIES

Other Realms I & II

I Heard it On the Radio

13 Bites III & IV

Plan 559 from Outer Space MK II & III

559 Ways to Die

Free For All

The Collapsar Directive

Relationship Add-Vice

Christmas Lites VII & VIII

Dedication:

This story is dedicated to children whose lives were changed forever by attending Indian schools. The children as they grew into adulthood suffered the effects of "Soul Wounds" with many individuals' feelings not worthy.

Native American lives today vary from productive to suicidal because of those disruptive years, and it's effect on the many generations that followed.

Acknowledgments

Thanks to everyone for all their hard work on this project. Couldn't do any of this without my beta readers, and faithful readers, thank you.

Hopefully, this story will assist people in understanding the plight of the Native American, and they will do research on their own. It is a part of history, we must never repeat.

You were never created to live
depressed, defeated, guilty,
condemned, ashamed or unworthy.
You were created to be
proud and victorious.
Author Unknown...

TABLE OF CONTENTS

Introduction:

I wrote this story to assist people in understanding the lasting effect Indian schools placed on different Native American tribes. At one time, over a hundred Indian boarding schools operated throughout this country. Thank goodness, Nevada's only school did not incur the severe abuse situations that many of the other schools created.

For over fifty years, Native American children from different tribes in the area **were forced to attend Indian Schools** in different States. The Stewart Indian school was open from 1890 to 1980. Ninety years in all, let that sink in...

The following, an excerpt from Andrea Smith, a survivor of an Indian school, may help you understand the deep wounds these boarding schools created**...**

"Soul Wound. The Legacy of Native American Schools"

"U.S. and Canadian authorities took Native American children from their homes and tried to civilize them through schools, sometimes trying to beat the Indian out them. Now

many years later, the Native Americans are dealing with the theft of their language, their culture, and of childhood itself."

+++

The destruction of Native American culture or family that occurred in the past, still carry these wounds today. These experiences clearly correlate with post-traumatic reactions, including social and psychological disruptions and breakdowns. Removing the children from their family broke the family bond and the traditional social structure of Indian communities. Before the Indian schools, native women generally enjoyed high status, according to scholars. Violence against women, children, and elders were virtually non-existent. Today, sexual abuse and violence along with alcoholism and suicide have reached epidemic proportions in many Native American communities. Many of the children succumbed to the wrong side of the white man's ways.

"The sexual assault rate among Native Americans is three-and-a-half times higher than for any other ethnic group in the U.S. Alcoholism is six times higher than the national average." (Bureau of Justice Statistics). Information has just begun to establish quantitative links between these epidemic rates from the legacy of Indian schools. Many more generations will pass before the damage from Indian Schools can be undone, if ever.

"The Stewart Indian School opened in 1890 and occupied 240 acres south of Carson City. Washoe, Paiute, and Shoshone and other various tribe's children were forced to attend. The Euro-American culture was taught to the children, who spent half of the day in the classroom learning English and mathematics, and the rest of the day receiving vocational training that often involved nothing more than doing work that was needed to maintain the school. Since the Indian boarding schools were under control of the War Department, the schools were run in a strict military style and focused on assimilation. Children as young as five years old were often rounded up and taken from their families while neither the children nor the parents knew what was happening. When they arrived at the school, they were forced to wear a uniform and to cut their hair. They were punished if they spoke their own languages. The children had a difficult time adjusting to the new strict environment and tried to run away.

They were almost always caught and brought back. Parents objected to having their children go to the school because they often became out of touch with their own culture and many of them never came home at all. There were high death rates at the schools due to epidemics of diseases such as influenza, smallpox, and cholera. Nearly all of the children reported suffering various amounts of psychological, physical and sexual abuse.

In later years the school was reported to have improved. The girls learned how to be a woman in white society and were trained in home economics and nursing. Boys were taught vocations usually designated for working-class white men like plumbing, carpentry, mechanics, and electrical work. Many graduates of the Stewart Indian School continued their education at other institutions, and many became prominent citizens in their communities by using the skills they had learned to help their people." (Stewart Indian School History)

This fiction story is about a young girl who grew up in the Indian school system and was taught to feel not worthy and the damaging effects of it on the road she chooses through adulthood. Her "Soul Wound" in seeking revenge.

Chapter One
September 1947

Tibe's world turned upside down the instant the Bureau of Indian Affairs (BIA) officers came to her home in Chiloquin, Oregon. They proceeded to inform her parents that Tibe was going to an Indian school in Nevada.

"It's best for her," they told her parents, "she will receive an education; better than what the tribe could offer. The training the child receives will help the tribe become successful in the future."

The officers insisted that with this education she would learn how to assimilate with civilized people. Besides, learning essential life skills that would benefit her, the family, and the tribe.

Joseph and Tibesa, Tibe's parents protested, but to no avail. *Joseph thought I can't lose my child, we have lost everything already. We have to live on this reservation, they have taken our land and our way of life, now they want our only child.* He had once been proud; Joseph was now a downtrodden, beaten man, what has become of us, of our tribe? These young officers didn't understand or care about the pain of them losing a child.

Tibe had turned six during the summer equinox and was still a young child in so many ways. Tibesa, held her hands to her face to hide her tears, Tibe needed the guidance and love of her parents and to know the history of her tribe.

"If she doesn't attend, we will stop any services you receive," stated one of the officers very firmly.

Regardless of whatever her parents said, Tibe knew she would end up going to the Indian School in Carson City. She fumed. Her little two-foot body tense with her heartbeat pounding, *ask me what I want,* she thought, as she clung to her Mother with angry tears in her eyes. The younger officer started to drag her away.

Tibesa stopped him and said to the child, "Tibe it will be all right, we will get you back, somehow." Then Tibesa turned to the officer and quietly said, "Let me packed a little knapsack of food and clothes for Tibe for the journey." He agreed.

The time came for her to go. Falgun, her black lab dog, came and licked her, he knew something was wrong. Tibe hugged him tight and asked the officer, "may he come too?"

The officer looked at her sadly and said quietly, "no."

Tibe gave the dog one more hug and said, "you stay boy," with tears in her eyes,

Tibe started to grab her Mother again, then dropped one of her arms, her skin tingled, and blood rushed through her limbs, quietly sobbing with pleading wild eyes, though still having one arm reaching toward her Mother as the officer took her away. Fury churned in Tibe's gut.

The young officer said with a smirk as they were leaving, "You can come and visit Tibe anytime and on holidays at your own expense." Falgun barked and showed his teeth as they took Tibe away.

Her parents hugged and cried together quietly after the officers took their only child. Where could they go to protest? Indians have no rights. They knew no one would listen. They had lost Tibe. Falgun laid down and whimpered, he knew too, she wasn't coming home.

+++

Tibe rode quietly to Nevada in the back seat of the car with three other children from her tribe. The ride was solemn, no one talked, and they all held hands for comfort. The children ages range from six to eight, they were scared as they had never been away from their parents or home. Now they only had each other for comfort.

The officer stopped once to let the children go to the bathroom, and if they wanted something to eat. All said no. Tibe had some venison jerky and smoked salmon in her knapsack which she shared. Tibe didn't eat as her stomach was soured with anger and sadness.

That windy September night, the scared, sad little six-year-old girl, who had never been away from her family arrived at the Indian boarding school in Nevada. From this point on, she would have no one to hug and love her or kiss away her fears. No one to tuck her in at night, or sing sweet lullabies to her... Tibe was all alone, Falgun wouldn't be sleeping with her. Her insides quivered. *I don't want to be here... Why didn't Dad put up a better fight?* Anger started building in her small body, her jaw tense and her skin tingling, as tears rolled down her tiny face. Tibe hated the whole world.

The girls slept in bunk beds in a barracks type room. There must have been twenty beds. She understood the boys' room was the same. Tibe's bed was in the last row at the far end of the room by a little window. She received a bottom bunk, probably because she was so small. She had a small box under her bed to put her things in, no lock, not that it was needed. This would be her home for the rest of her life... She slams her little fists on the bed. *I am important! No one cares because I am a young Indian, a savage... Do they think, I have no feelings? Someday, they will see.*

+++

Tibe and the other children from different tribes saw their life changed that first week dramatically at the school.

First, their beautiful black hair was cut short (a source of shame for the boys). Tibe's long straight hair, had never been cut, was shortened to shoulder length. The children were forced to wear uniforms. Tibe had to wear a plain cotton skirt, and blouse, no more buckskin or animal fur.

All the children received English names. Tibe David, her name at birth, meaning the moon and sun became Joann David. Plus, the food they had to eat at the school differed from their diet at home. Many children grew sick from the diet change, including Joann. Joann had never eaten meat like this, she spent days in the bathroom throwing up or worse. She swore they were trying to poison her. Tibe's chest tightened, her throat scratched with thirst, but she wasn't thirsty, just angry. Life changed so drastically in just a week.

Nonetheless, the one thing the kids knew that wouldn't change, was that they would attend this school for the rest of their young lives or die here. They would never again, live with their parents, they had to survive this ordeal.

Joann was not allowed to speak her own language, even among members of her own tribe. If she did, and they caught her, they would wash her mouth with lye soap. Oh, how Joann hated this school and what it represented. She was a caged animal and wanted to go home to be with her parents. Her only crime was being an Indian.

Many long, lonely nights Joann cried herself very quietly to sleep. She never ever let anyone see this weak side. She's a proud Indian! All two and a half feet of her.

The children attending the school had to go to church services and were strongly encouraged to convert to Christianity. It was not of interest to Joann, she had her Creator, Mother Earth. The school's harsh disciplinary rules were no more than in their own families. They were about doing chores, misbehavior, and schoolwork. However, here if the child slacked off, they would face harsh punishment, such as no dinner or a beating with a wooden paddle. The amount of punishment varied depending on the crime or the mood of the teacher.

Joann existed in a situation where her views seemed in opposition to those in charge. Because of this, it became necessary for her to keep her beliefs and anger private. Joann quickly learned to do what was expected of her, such as her homework and her chores and remained in the graces of the teachers. She became like the deer in the forest, very perceptive and observant, never missing a thing going on around her. She learned to go unnoticed and disappear instantly.

Nevertheless, her anger kept building inside her each day and sometimes it was hard to hide. One day in the bakery, when no one was around, anger rose in her tightening chest. She tore a loaf of bread into little pieces screaming on the inside. She was so angry, sweat trickled down her spine. After she calmed down, she quickly realized what she had done and took the bread out to the chickens, to eat to hide the crime. She felt blessed that she never got caught.

+++

During the following years, Joann learned how to type, read, and write in English. She learned the basics of cooking and sewing her own clothes. The school's policy; trained the girls to grow up to become good wives and mothers so they will assimilate their children in a civilized manner. Teach them white man's ways. It's a form of brainwashing by the government. Even young Joann saw through the ruse, being the deer, she missed nothing. Her hatred of this life and the school just kept growing and building like a volcano. One day it was going to blow. Besides, no one, including Joann, knew when or how it might end. She would patiently wait for her chance to get even...someday.

Chapter Two
The Year 1953

Six long years passed since Joann came to Stewart. She saw her parents about a year ago, and it broke her heart when they left. Her parents still lived on the reservation in Oregon. Work was extremely limited for her Dad, and her Mother, who now suffered from breast cancer, making it financially hard for them to come and visit.

In the past six years, she learned to adapt to the white man's way, go to their church, but she still prayed to her creator. She became a chameleon, did as she was told and was a model student.

A sad Joann sat on her bed celebrating her twelfth birthday. Her parents had sent her a birthday card. They write all the time and sent what little money they could for her birthdays and Christmas.

She sat there thinking, *Why am I treated unworthily affection or happiness? Why can't I be with my parents on my birthday?* And the tears flowed from her dark piercing eyes down her sad face.

Joann had hardened her feelings over the years, as she trusted no one. She makes her emotional wall so high from all the hate that she didn't make friends easily; she felt they'd let her down like her parents.

In this state of mind, she couldn't understand why she didn't deserve to be loved or liked. Being separated from family, it must be her fault... *like heck it is, it is this school!* And the tears flowed again, hot this time. Heat rolled in her guts.

It was a lonely birthday for a twelve-year-old girl, to be by herself, with no close friends or family to help her celebrate. A lump formed in her throat. Joann even baked her own birthday cupcake. She quietly eats it and cries. *Someday, I will make things go right for me, I will show them, I will get even. I am important, I am someone! This became her mantra.*

Joann hated this government who thought up this school? Who is cruel enough not to allow her to live with her family and tribe? She lived for the day when she would go home. It was all she could think of, it possessed her. Joann spat to clear her clogged throat of hate.

+++

Joann wasn't a girl that stood out, her five feet-two-inch small body reeked of shyness. She wore her dark hair in a long braid or sometimes in ponytails, which emphasized her light olive complexion and high cheekbones. The most noticeable thing about Joann was her dark piercing, sad, cold brown eyes, always alert, observing everything.

The years of mental abuse, her loneliness, and her culture, Joann entered a room, slipping in and out. *Don't get noticed.* But, inside, she hated being alone. She wanted to feel needed, but she didn't know how to obtain affection or friendship.

Joann never shared her feelings with anyone, even her parents. Joann felt her parents wouldn't understand her misery or that maybe her parents might also be miserable. In her mind, the school had taught her, she wasn't worthy of anyone loving her, including her parents.

Joann also was frustrated over not truly knowing her parents anymore. She'd been gone for six years! Joann kept a family picture, of her Mom, Dad, and her dog to help her on those lonely nights, remembering the few fun memories she had with them. The sad part she was so young when she left, she only had a few memories. Her Dad taking her fishing, her Mom teaching her how to swim, and her dog, Falgun, meaning Spring, she so missed him, he would cuddle with her. Her Mom said he passed last year, and Joann wasn't there to say goodbye, the tears came again, this time hot from anger.

She put the picture under her pillow and slept on it. Joann's heart was broken from the loss of her family. *Will I ever live with them again? Nonetheless, she knew the family bond wasn't there anymore, they were like strangers.*

+++

Yet, through all of her shyness, Joann was noticed by one of her teachers.

+++

One school day, Mr. Simmons, her history teacher, asked as the class was breaking up, "Joann would you stay after class, I wanted to discuss a problem with you?"

Joann became concerned, and the back of her throat ached, and she struggled to swallow, she stammered, " Did I do something wrong, Mr. Simmons?"

"Oh no, I just want to go over this report with you," as he walked to the back of the room and locked the door. He came back up to her, too close; in fact, and grabbed her quickly, putting his hand over her mouth, knocking her to the ground, pressing his over two hundred pounds on her, as she went down. Joann's heart pounded and a ball of fear formed in her stomach, what is happening?

Joann tried to scream. However, he hit her hard, splitting her lip and pushing all eighty pounds of her down to the floor, beating her head to the floor, knocking her out. At the young age of twelve, Mr. Larry Simmons beat and raped her.

+++

After the incident, the school nurse, Mrs. Louise Bush, took care of her injuries. Joann never saw a hospital as she was lucky she hadn't broken anything. She never talked to the police or the school Dean as Mrs. Bush told Joann not to speak of the incident, or things would be worse for her. Joann thought *I'd never talk about what happened to me, to anyone,* as *anger rolled in her gut. I'll get even!* Mrs. Bush said, "I'll take care of this issue and make sure nothing like this ever happens to you again, Joann."

Good to her word, nothing like that ever occurred again. Over the rest of the year, Mr. Simmons ignored Joann like she didn't exist. Thank goodness, she didn't have to take any more classes with him, Mrs. Bush saw to that. Nevertheless, she planned her revenge down to the last details. Joann now had someone to focus all those years of anger on. She started planning on how she would get even, no matter how long it took. Joann had the patience and the skills to be quiet and deadly. She had a goal. She had a face to put on that anger and hate.

+++

Shortly after the incident with Mr. Simmons, Joann took a real interest in home economics, as this was the first part of her revenge plan. In a short period, she excelled at cooking desserts, thanks to classes taught by Alma Daly, a friendly stout woman in her late forties.

This time became the best experience in Joann's young life. Alma taught Joann how to become an excellent cook and how to sew clothes to look like they came from the store. The two became good friends or as close as anyone ever got to Joann. Joann thought of Alma like the grandmother-type, mainly because of Alma's pre-mature gray hair. Joann barely remembered her real grandma, who had passed away several years ago, while she was in this darn school. However, Joann remembers her Grandma's loving smile and her gray hair. Alma always has that same smile.

Alma also taught Joann, how to quilt, a specialty of Alma's. Joann was a fast learner and in no time was making beautiful quilts that sold at the Wa-Pai-Shone Trading Post. Many students place products on display for the general public to buy. The extra money from the sale of the quilts gave her the ability to purchase more material and send some money to her parents. Her mother's illness still prevailed.

The first hug Joann received since leaving her parents, over six years ago came from Mrs. Daly when Joann baked a birthday cake for Alma's birthday party. She made her a three-tier-chocolate cake, which looked and tasted fabulous. Joann made it with all the affection she could for Mrs. Daly. Joann didn't know what it's like to love someone, but she cared a lot for Mrs. Daly. Yet, her anger was still simmering beneath the surface which held her back from trusting anyone else. Still, she thought *I am Tibe, I am somebody, and I am worthy...*

+++

Over time, her classmates, and teachers began to rave about Joann's baking abilities. Joann made cakes, cookies, and muffins that melted in your mouth. She shared her creations will all, just to receive their positive feedback. Joann was pleased with the kind words she received, *people really liked her desserts.*

Joann took orders through the store from customers who enjoyed her baked goods. In fact, the store had to create a waiting list for her goodies. Joann became proud of her accomplishments, and her heart bubbled with joy. *I am somebody.* Alma took some pictures of Joann handiwork, and Joann sent them to her parents, with cookies and extra money. They beamed with pride and shared her cookies with friends. Her parents were proud to be part of their daughter's life, even if only by mail.

Chapter Three
The year 1955

Finally came the day, Joann now fourteen, that she felt her cooking surpassed her expectations. She became good enough to share her desserts with her favorite teacher Mr. Simmons. *How she hated him*. She planned this event for well over a year on how she would achieve her revenge. The skills of a snake... deadly patience.

+++

Late Friday afternoon, right before a warm three-day weekend. She watched and waited for the perfect time. Then she snuck into Mr. Simmons's classroom while he went to the bathroom. She left a plate of chocolate chip cookies with raisins on his desk for him. It had a note, "To the teacher who is most deserving of these cookies."

When Mr. Simmons returned, he smiled from ear to ear, being pleased that someone had given him a couple dozen big cookies with such a sweet note. He thought, *bet it's that Indian squaw, Joann. Maybe she liked what I did to her....* Mr. Simmons loved sweets, and his five-foot-ten-inch body showed it. He loved chocolate and being hungry, he gobbled three, then the fourth cookie right away. *Unknown to him, Joann had laced the cookies with poison.* Thirty minutes later, as he prepared to leave for home, he started not feeling well. He thought, *great coming down with something I caught from these Indian brats and damn, I have a three-day weekend,* as he walked out the door to his car with his cookies. He ate another cookie, and it made him feel better. *That's the problem. I'm just hungry.*

Mr. Simmons lived about a mile from the school. *This type of poison can cause severe convulsions, usually within a short time after ingestion.* Larry started throwing up shortly after he got home. Then he felt a slight tightness in the chest. Larry began having difficulty breathing and notice an irregular heartbeat, plus a dry cough. He thought *should I call the Doctor.*

Nevertheless, after a few minutes, the chest pain started to ease up. *Oh, I am all right. I just caught a bug from those damn heathens.*

Larry didn't feel like cooking, so grabbing a handful of cookies and a glass of milk from the kitchen, he went into the front room, to sit in his chair and read the paper. As he sat there eating cookies and drinking his milk, he found he couldn't concentrate on reading the article. He felt fatigued. Within no time, he fell asleep in his recliner. Larry lived alone, in fact, he didn't even have a pet.

The next morning, getting up out of his recliner; he couldn't believe he slept there all night. He went to the bathroom for his morning pee and notices some blood in his urine. "What the heck," and he felt like crap. *Maybe I should call the Doctor. Oh hell, it's a three-day weekend, everyone will be gone,* and he didn't want to go to the ER. He brushed his teeth, and blood showed on his toothbrush. Not a lot, just a little. *Darn, must have cut myself,* he thought, *but on what?*

Larry went into the kitchen and made some coffee, and just that little effort exhausted him. He poured himself a cup and grabbed a few more cookies while he sat at the kitchen table, still trying to read yesterday's paper. His hands and feet seemed cold. *Well, even though it was warm, you slept with no blanket, you idiot. I think I will go to bed, I am just not feeling well.* He staggered down the hall and went into the guest room instead of his bedroom. *What is wrong with me? He headed back toward his bedroom.*

Larry crawled into bed and turned on the clock radio. He had brought the remaining cookies and another cup of coffee with him. After eating a few more cookies, he starting thinking *these are great cookies,* again wondering who gave them to him? After eating the last of the cookies, he again fell fast asleep. It was late in the afternoon when he finally woke up. Larry being weak, staggering to the bathroom, again blood in his urine, more this time. He looked in the mirror, and there's blood on his face from his mouth. His color was pale and almost yellow. Suddenly, Larry started throwing up, and he couldn't stop, he fell to the floor in exhaustion from dry heaves. Larry tried, but he couldn't get up, and now there was blood everywhere. The last thing Larry remembers, *I need to call an ambulance.*

Chapter Four

Tuesday morning, Mr. Simmons didn't show up for work, and he didn't answer his phone. Mr. George Hunter, the Principal, became concerned. Larry may not be the best teacher because he has an attitude toward the kids, but darn it, he has a job and needs to do it. *If sick, he should have called in. Nevertheless, not showing up for work, in my book, is unacceptable behavior. Now I'll have to find a sub to take his place. All of this creates more work for me. Damn. I'll go to his house later, check on him, and give him a piece of my mind for not calling in.* Mr. Hunter's philosophy of "going by the book" made this behavior not acceptable.

+++

Joann looked for Mr. Simmons, and wondered if the cookies work? Did they make him sick? She didn't know how much rat poison would do the trick, so she had given him the whole bottle.

+++

Finally, around two in the afternoon, when things slowed down, George went to check on Larry. He drove up to his house, Larry's car was parked in the driveway. George knocked several times on the door, no answer. He tried the handle; the door was locked. *Alright, Larry, where are you??* George walked around to the side of the house and looked in, no sign of Larry or any activity anywhere. *Well, damn, guess he went somewhere and didn't tell us. I know he's got plenty of vacation leave, and with the three-day weekend and all.* With that, George left Larry's house very upset. *Damn, Larry should have let me know he wasn't coming in. I'll call him and leave a message telling him what I think.*

When George got back to his office, he made the call to Larry's and left a message on the answering machine, giving him heck for not showing up and not calling. Since it was Tuesday, George gave him a three-day suspension unless he showed back up with a good reason for missing work. This meant Larry better show up at work next Monday or else.

For the next few days, Joann looked for Mr. Simmons, but he never came to work. She asked Mrs. Daly if she knew anything. Who replied, "no and it is none of our business." Alma didn't like Mr. Simmons. She didn't like how he treated the children, especially young girls. Alma didn't understand why he hadn't been fired.

Monday came and still no Mr. Simmons. Joann became worried now, she wanted to make him very sick with those cookies. She wondered what had happened. He hadn't shown up for ten days. Then she thought, *well, whatever happened to him, he deserved it for what he did to me,* and with that, she let it go.

Wednesday, Principal Hunter announced that Mr. Simmons had died and Mr. Louis Black would take his place. Joann seemed pleasantly surprised he died. *Well, the poison actually worked. That was easy, maybe too easy. She only wanted to make him sick.*

Nevertheless, she thought, *he deserved what he got.* Rumors had it that the house was full of blowflies because of the body and the heat. The medics were throwing up getting the body out of the house. *Couldn't have happened to a better person.*

Joann had killed her enemy. She felt no remorse, only joy. She had her revenge. He had stolen her womanhood, and no one suspected her of killing him. At that moment, life had changed for her. She could control her own life, maybe not her destiny, but, she could get revenge because she was worthy.

Chapter Five
The Year 1957

On Saturdays, Joann could take her pass and go into Carson City to shop for the day. Indians only travel on Saturdays unless they worked an after-school job. Even then, they better arrive back to the school when the six p.m. whistle/alarm goes off, or there's heck to pay.

Joann rarely went to town, as the school, was about three miles from town. Moreover, if she did go to town, it was only on occasion usually with Mrs. Daly. Sometimes one of her other female teachers might give her a lift. Joann never traveled with a male teacher, as she didn't trust any of them.

Today, however, is different, Joann's parents sent her some money for her sixteenth birthday. Plus, what she saved from selling her quilts, she could buy material for new clothes.

Joann usually rode the bus to the bus station in Carson City. Today, however, she got a ride with Mrs. Daly. Alma said she would pick Joann up at five-thirty. Joann smiled seeing this saved her a whole dollar. This day began as her lucky day.

There's an excellent fabric-clothing store in town where Joann buys her fabric. They always have a good selection of material and clothes. Joann could never afford to buy clothes there, as it was not in her budget. By sewing her own clothes, she saved money. After purchasing the lovely materials she liked, she had over a dollar to spend, which would have paid for the bus ride home. However, getting a ride from Alma, it gave her extra money. *I can splurge.*

Joann decided to celebrate by walking quickly down to the Penguin Drive-in to purchase an ice cream cone. She sat at the outside table, eating her ice cream cone, enjoying the weather. Two white boys about her age came by; they ordered hamburgers and fries and asked if they could share the table with her. One of them was cute, tall and muscular, probably a football player. *What could it hurt*, she thought. "Sure, there's plenty of room," she stammered with her head lowered.

"Hi, my name is Claude, and he's Roger, what's yours?"

"Joann," she replied, blushing, still not looking up.

"You new here? As I haven't seen you at school," asked Claude

Joann thought for a moment, "Yes, We just moved here, I haven't started school yet." She couldn't believe how easy it was to talk to them... She looked at both of them in their eyes.

She was amazing herself, it's like she became a different person. *I am as good as you...*

The three of them talked for a while, and finally, though she hated to, she said, "I have to leave, nice meeting you both."

Both boys stood up and said, "Nice meeting you and hope to see you around the school."

Joann started walking back toward the middle of town while they watched her leave. Joann thought *I like Claude, he's nice, and I hope I see him again. Best yet, he doesn't know I attend Stewart Indian School. He thinks I am a regular kid...*

+++

Nevertheless, Joann did get to see Claude again, many weeks later on a Friday night at the football game. Of course, she couldn't talk to him, they just waved at each other, but now he knows she goes to Stewart Indian School. Joann didn't go back to town for a couple of months, she was too embarrassed. *Why can't I be like everyone else? I am an Indian, and I am proud of it, not ashamed. Why have they made me feel so unworthy?*

Over the next couple of years, she saw Claude from a distance, but she never talked to him, maybe someday.

Chapter Six
The Year 1959

The time finally passed. Joann turned eighteen and graduated from Stewart, she was free of that school and that life. Yet, out on her own, she became lonely and missed what few friends she had made. *Though she thought, I will never miss that school.* Most of the students that graduated went back to their families.

In Joanne case, both of her parents had died in a car accident last year while she was still in school. Due to cost, she wasn't able to go to their funeral. Nevertheless, so much time had passed, she felt she really didn't know her parents anymore anyway. She grieved, but it was short-lived. She didn't know her Aunts and Uncles. In fact, she didn't know any of her family, so she decided to stay in Carson.

With age and time, some of her anger had dissipated. Nonetheless, after so many years, it still lurked under the surface. Being around Alma had been good for her concerning her anger. Alma was teaching her that life was good.

Joann obtained a job with the State of Nevada Highway Department. She became a secretary in the Planning Division. It was a great job, she worked with two older women, who treated her like their daughter.

Alma offered to let Joann stay with her, which Joann accepted. "Saying she would only stay until she had enough money to rent her own apartment."

She paid a small amount of rent and help clean Alma's house. They shared their meals and cooking. The relationship worked well for both of them. Alma was the closest thing to family Joann had, and she cared a lot for her.

After a couple of months, Joann found a lovely little apartment on Curry Street. Joann decorated it with things she made, and what Alma gave her. She even got a little kitten, which she named Mr. Bojangles. He was black and white with a cute looking bow tie under his chin. For the first time, Joann had something to love that was hers. She had thought about a dog, but the landlord didn't allow them, so the cat would do.

Joann still sold her quilts at the Indian store for extra money. After working for six months, Joann was able to buy herself a car, a used two-door blue 1950 Chevy. Between rent, car payment and living expense, she was limited on what she could do for fun. So she cooked desserts and sold them at a local bakery for extra money. Life was good and busy for her, and everyone loved her desserts.

Joann was lonely, and she still had trouble meeting and trusting people, but she had Mr. Bojangles and Mrs. Daly. Basically, Alma was Joann's family, and Joann was hers. Alma's husband had died a few years back, and they never had any children.

Joann still thought, *Why do I still feel not worthy... well, for one thing, you are Indian, you are not like the rest.* She would argue with herself. Joann never gave herself any credit, or in fact, anyone else. Because of her youth, she always thought the worst. Her anger, although hidden most of the time, didn't let her see anyone else's problems, just hers.

+++

On some Saturday summer nights, Joann would go to the movies alone. If she felt like it, she might even go bowling afterward at Berger's Alley. Berger's bowling alley only had six lanes, but it was fun. Sometimes, she would run into people she worked with at the Highway Department. On this particular night at the theater, she was buying popcorn before entering the movie, and she heard a voice behind her say, "Hi, Joann, long time no see."

She turned around, and there stood Claude. She didn't know what to say, she lowered her head and blushed, "Why hi, how are you, Claude? *He's even better looking now that he's grown up. He'd let his hair grow a little longer with sideburns.*

"Fine. Are you with someone? Or can we sit together during the movie?" He asked. Claude thought as he was looking at Joann, *she has changed; she is cuter with a sweet smile and those sad piercing brown eyes.*

Joann hesitated before answering with her head still lowered, "That's OK, I understand," Claude said.

"Sorry. No, I would love to sit with you," she stammered.

Claude beamed, "Great. That will be great."

They watched "North to Alaska" with John Wayne and then they both went bowling. It was a great night. Claude asked if he could see her again and they set up a time and a place to meet. She didn't want him to see her apartment, not yet. They decided to meet next Friday night at the Carson Nugget for dinner then take in a movie, "Flaming Star" with Elvis Presley. They both liked Presley. He walked her to the Nugget parking lot, gave her a hug, "See you next Friday. It will be a long week waiting to see you again."

Joann blushed, "See you then." Moreover, she gave him a big smile as she hopped into her car and drove home. Her heart drummed a fast dance, she was so excited. If she were walking, she would have skipped all the way home.

+++

Joann, couldn't wait until Friday. Finally, Friday came. She tried on several outfits getting ready for the date. She ended up wearing a floral dress, with a blue sweater to show off her brown eyes. She had curled her hair in ringlets. After looking at herself in the mirror, "This is as good as it gets, I hope he's not disappointed." Joann knew she wasn't beautiful but was sweet and pleasant to be around. She had become a good listener over the years. She remembered everything Claude said to her. Joann was the happiest she has ever been in her life. Yet, she was also cautious; *be careful Joann... you are Indian.* With that, she went on her way to the Nugget for her date with Claude.

They both ordered Awful-Awful's, which is a big hamburger with fries, and a coke. Dinner was great, they talked about everything. Claude told her he's a sophomore at the University of Nevada in Reno. He wanted to be a football coach and was now playing on the University of Nevada Wolf Pack football team as a tight end. Joann told him about her job. He listened and asked questions.

The movie wasn't Elvis's best. Nevertheless, Joann was happy to be with Claude and didn't care what they saw. She's

was sitting next to Claude, and he wanted to be with her...
Joann's heart bubbled with joy.

+++

They continued this ritual for several weeks, having dinner, and seeing a show. After seeing "Swiss Family Robinson," they slow-walked back to the Nugget. Claude asked her, "Joann, would like to go on a picnic on Sunday?"

"I think that would be fun, where would we go?" Responded Joann.

"Have you ever been to Lake Tahoe?"

"Once several years ago, but never on a picnic," stated Joann.

"Then we are on. I'll pick you up at eleven, and bring a bathing suit. However, the water is freezing."

"I'll meet you here at the Nugget, is that good?"

"Yeah, but don't you think maybe, I can pick you up at your house?"

Joann thought about it, "Soon, but not at this time."

Claude hung his head, "Okay for now." He again gave her a hug and a slight kiss on her cheek and said, "Goodnight Joann, see you on Sunday."

"See you then," she drove to her apartment. Her mind was a whirl. I don't have a bathing suit... Therefore, I must go

41

clothes shopping tomorrow. Warmth spread through Joann's limbs, this was the happiest she had ever been...

+++

After doing all her chores, it was late Saturday afternoon when she went shopping for a bathing suit at Beverly's. She never had a bathing suit before. Joann found a single piece, black with white ruffles. She looked good in the suit, but she felt embarrassed. It was so revealing. She bought a large shirt to wear over it, and that made her feel a little better.

Suddenly there was a knock on the door, "You need to come out this instant," said the voice with a growl. Joann had heard the owner would walk in on you, but this was a woman's voice.

"I will be right there, let me put my clothes back on," as she was pulling up her skirt. The door opened, "You must leave the store now," demanded the clerk with a scowl on her face.

"Why?"

"You're Indian, it's almost six; you must leave now," demanded the voice.

"I graduated. I don't have to be back at the school," as she dug through her purse to find her ID. Joann was fuming, but she kept control of herself. *How dare this woman...what gave her the right?*

"Get out, get out now, or I will call the authorities," yelled the clerk.

"Call them, I am legal," Joann was now mad, she had never spoken up before, but she was so angry. "I'll pay for my bathing suit, and then I'll leave," she said through gritted teeth and clenched fists.

The store clerk was taken back. "I am calling the authorities now," and stomped off.

Joann finished getting dressed, gathered her stuff, and stormed out to the cash register, put her money down to pay for the bathing suit and said to the clerk, "I'll wait for the authorities." Joann couldn't believe how calm, she became, *I am worthy, I did my time, I'll be treated like everyone else...* "Is this how you treat your customers?" Joann quietly asked the girl behind the counter, whose name was Marcy according to her lapel pin.

"Just dumb Indians," Marcy snarled. Joann didn't say another word, just gripped her purse hard. *Keep calm, don't hit her... Joann's jaw ached from anger.*

A few minutes later, a police officer came in and asked what was going on. The clerk told him that Joann was Indian and was to be gone by six p.m. and it was now after six. Joann showed the officer her ID and that she had graduated from the school and works for the Highway Department. "I just want to pay for my bathing suit and go home," she stated very calmly.

The officer told the clerk, "Marcy, ring this lady up and quit harassing your customers," and walked out of the store.

The clerk was visibly upset, but she never said she was sorry. She rang up Joann's suit and again snarled, "Indian, next time take your business somewhere else." *What a bitch,* thought Joann with her anger steaming.

Joann talked to herself all the way home; she was so embarrassed... Joann was outraged! *Who did that clerk think she was? I'll get even with her someday, and the revenge will be sweet. Marcy, you have met your match.*

Chapter Seven

Sunday came, and Joann was waiting by her car for Claude at the Nugget parking lot. She packed a lunch. Joann made several large ham and cheese sandwiches and baked two dozen peanut butter cookies. She could hardly stand still from the excitement; she was going to Lake Tahoe with Claude for the day! Life couldn't get any better.

"Hey you, ready to go"? As he walked up behind her and gave her a hug.

"Yes sir," she replied a little startled, "This is going to be a beautiful day. I packed us a lunch."

"That is great, I bought some drinks. We will be meeting some friends, hope you don't mind. Do you remember Roger?" Asked Claude.

"Barely, but that will be great," replied Joann, though she didn't really like crowds.

"He is bringing his girlfriend, I think you will like her, she's quiet like you," he said laughingly.

They got into his green and white 1955 Chevy Impala and off they went to the Lake. He was telling her they were going to Sand Harbor. It's where everybody goes swimming.

"We could go to a nude beach," he said smiling looking at her.

"I don't think so," said Joann smiling back at him. She thought *I feel so comfortable with Claude, he accepts me for what I am.*

The time flew as they drove up the mountain. For Joann a day with Claude and meeting his friends was exciting. This is what ordinary people do, and he must like me if he wants me to meet his friends. The day was warm, and the sand felt good on her feet as they walked from the car to a picnic table. The Lake was just a stone throw from the table. Lake Tahoe is a beautiful high sierra mountain lake; it is so clear, and blue. One of the natural wonders of the world, she couldn't wait to jump in.

"Hey you two, you guys beat us here," came a voice from behind them. It was Roger and his girlfriend. Joann froze; her throat closed, it was that girl "Marcy" from the store. The one that called the police on her. Joann didn't know what to do. She didn't say a word and tried to slide into the woodwork. Maybe the girl won't remember her.

"This is Marcy, my girlfriend," said Roger.

"This is Joann; you remember her, right, Rodger?" Stated Claude.

Roger said, " Sure. Hi. Joann, this is Marcy."

"I have met... Joann... before," sneered Marcy.

"Really, where?" inquired Claude. Claude looked at Joann with a question on his face.

"Oh, it is a long story, and it doesn't matter," Marcy interrupted. Joann didn't say anything. She just wanted to crawl away. Joann hated this girl, but she was not going to let her ruin her day with Claude.

"Fancy that, you two know each other. Well, that is good," stated Claude as he hugged Joann.

The afternoon went by slowly. Finally, everyone started to loosen up after drinking a few beers. Joann said, "I have sandwiches and cookies." She opened up her basket, and everyone dug in. "These cookies are really great," they all chimed.

"I didn't know...Ind...you could cook," commented Marcy.

Joann stared at her with cold eyes and started to say something when Roger sensed a problem and said, "Let's go swimming. I need the cold water to clear my head." With that, he went running into the water. Claude followed him. Joann and Marcy were left still sitting on the picnic bench.

"I see you are wearing the suit you bought. Shall we go try it out, or did you just wear it to get laid by Claude?" Marcy asked with a sneer.

"What?" Joann didn't know what to say, *what a b----, why would she say such a thing...* Before Joann could answer, Marcy ran off into the water.

After a second or two, Joann ran into the water also, when she was up to her waist, the cold water hit her. *Criminy the water is cold, she* thought. Marcy was already out swimming with the guys. Not to be outdone, Joann swam out to join them, her teeth chattering.

"See you back on the beach," said Claude as the guys started to head back to shore, saying they had enough of this cold water.

Joann and Marcy were swimming close by each other, when Marcy snarled, "I didn't think dumb Injuns knew how to swim?" Joann looked at her and anger swelled up inside. Joann's neck stiffened, and her chest grew tight.

"What is your problem, Marcy?" asked Joann. However, before Marcy could answer, Joann thought *I'll show her a thing or two.* Joann checked and saw that the guys were back on shore, with that she, dove under the water, teeth clench, and headbutted Marcy in her stomach so hard it knocked the air out of Marcy. *That's for calling me a dumb Injun.*

Quickly, Joann turned and swam back to shore. *The b--- - thought Joann.* Joann got back to the beach and looked for Marcy, she wasn't behind her... *good, hope she drowned.* Then Joann thought, *oh crap! I better get help,* she started yelling at the guys, telling them Marcy didn't follow her back and she doesn't see her. Both of the guys jumped in the water and started looking for Marcy, with no success. Joann ran down the shore about a hundred yards to a lifeguard and told him what was happening.

Everything was happening so fast. The guard jumped on a Ski-Doo and came over to the guys, they were still diving down looking for Marcy. A few minutes went by, seemed like hours before they brought up Marcy's body. The guys quickly put her body on the back of the Ski-Doo and brought her to shore. The lifeguard started giving her mouth to mouth resuscitation, but to no avail. Marcy was dead.

Serves her right, thought Joann. Joann sat on the beach with no emotions, just in shock or so they thought. Claude came over with a towel and wrapped it around her, "You alright?"

"It's my fault, I should have swum in with her," stammered Joann.

"It wasn't anyone's fault, the water is cold, she probably cramped," exclaimed Claude as he hugged Joann. Joann leaned in on the hug and his warmth and though *if you only knew. Marcy will never be able to make me feel, not worthy again... the b----.*

Marcy's body was taken to Carson City by ambulance. She and Claude followed it down behind Roger, who was right at the back of the ambulance. The day was ruined. They didn't talk on the way off the mountain. Claude dropped her off at her car and said he would call her. Joann was upset because the day was ruined, but she had no remorse for dead Marcy. She argued with herself, *I have to learn to control my temper, I could have been seen today. Marcy had no right to make me feel not worthy...* And the argument when on like that all the way home and until she went to bed.

Chapter Eight

It wasn't until next Friday when she saw Claude again in the movie theater. He didn't say anything as he sat down beside her. Joann couldn't even remember what she was watching; she just knew she had to leave. As she got up and started walking out of the theater, Claude followed her. They still hadn't spoken.

She started walking home, with Claude, besides her. Finally, he commented, "Joann everything will be ok, I promise. It wasn't anyone's fault."

Joann stopped and looked at him "Everything is my fault. I am Indian," she stated angrily. Claude grabbed and shook her, "You may be Indian, but Marcy drowning was not your fault, and you know it."

"I have been taught, everything is my fault, since I was six," shouted Joann, *she was amazed she could lie to Claude... It was her fault, she had gladly killed Marcy.*

They walked some more without talking, and they suddenly appeared in front of her apartment. She hadn't planned on that, but there they were. She had to ask Claude inside.

"Would you like to come into my home?"

"Yes, I would. Thank you for asking me." They talked as they walked into her place, "everything is going to be okay. Roger is handling it quite well. The funeral was last Thursday. He and I got drunk afterward."

"I feel for him," Joann stated maybe a little too coldly.

"Truth be known, he was going to break up with her, as she wasn't really nice to his friends,"

No shit thought Joann. "Would you like a drink or some coffee?"

"Beer if you have one?"

"Sure do," and they both sat down on the couch with a beer. "You have a cute place here," as Mr. Bojangles jumped up on the couch to see the visitor. "What's the cat's name?"

"Mr. Bojangles." And they both laughed. Mr. Bojangles checked Claude out, turned his nose up and left. They laugh again.

"Guess the cat doesn't like me."

"He just not used to strangers." Though Joann thought it was odd.

One thing led to another and Claude spent the night with her. She was in heaven. He hugged and kissed her and made her feel like she was worthy... quite worthy.

Chapter Nine

The summer flew by, Joann had never been so happy. She felt like she finally belonged and was loved. She and Claude were inseparable. They did everything together. He took her to the State Fair in Reno, and she rode the Ferris wheel. He won her a big teddy bear. They went to the rodeo, went camping, and did things she had never done or seen before, She saw life through Claude's eyes. This was what regular people did that she had never been allowed to participate or enjoy. Life was too good to be true.

With summer coming to an end, Claude would be going back to college. He was already doing football conditioning, getting ready for the season. But they agreed they would spend every weekend together. She would come to all the home games.

The weekend before he went back to school, Claude told her he loved her, and when he finished college, they would get married. Joann pinched herself, she couldn't believe life could be this good.

However, around Easter, Joann's life changed again. She found out she was pregnant. *How am I going to tell Claude? How will he react?*

The following Saturday night, she had cooked an excellent meal and talked about the week. As they were sitting on the couch drinking a beer, Joann said, "Claude I have some news you might not like to hear."

He looked at her with a sad face, "You are breaking up with me?"

"No silly, but I am not sure how you will take the news," explained Joann.

"Well, what is it?" Claude asked.

"I am going to have a visitor in October," she said coyly.

"Great I will get to meet some of your family?" He asked.

"Our family," and she let that sink in...

Claude looked at her with a questioning look, "You mean..."

"Yes, a baby in October," explained Joann.

He grabbed and hugged her hard, "we will just get married sooner."

Joann was ecstatic that he was happy about it.

Claude started pacing the floor, "I need to tell my parents, and let's plan an Easter wedding."

"Wow, slow down a bit. Are you sure this is what you want to do?" Asked Joann.

"Yes," he said very forcefully. "We'll tell my parents tomorrow when we'll go to visit them."

"I have never met your parents," Joann murmured, "what if they don't like me?"

"They will love you." as he hugged her again "because I love you."

+++

On Sunday Joann got dressed in her best work outfit, she was so nervous, what if they don't like her. *She was an Indian after all, not worthy of a man like Claude. Quit being silly. If they are Claude parents, they will like me.* However, there was a knot in her stomach. I am going to become Mrs. Claude Stone, she kept telling herself.

Claude showed up around noon, and off to Yerington, they went to see his parents. His parents had moved to Yerington several years ago to live on a ranch. Joann was shaking when they arrived at their home. It was a mansion. The house was three stories high, with lions on each side of the steps leading up to the front door. *Oh, shit... They are wealthy to boot. This is not going to go well, I can feel it.*

Claude's mother, Edith met them at the door with a scowl on her face. She shut the door behind her, and snarled at Joann, "I need to talk to Claude for a moment, do you mind?"

"No... no, I don't mind," stammered Joann as she sheepishly walked back down the steps and stood by the car. Claude said nothing.

Joann watched as Claude's Mom, and he had words. Then his Dad, Anthony, came staggering out. It wasn't pleasant, they were having an argument right there on the front porch. Thank goodness there were no close neighbors.

Joann couldn't hear everything they said, but the general drift was you are not marrying an Indian... "If you marry her, I will disown you," stated his Father. Claude looked down at Joann, and he was almost in tears. Joann couldn't take it anymore and ran off.

She walked to the next ranch house and asked to use a phone. Joann called a cab to take her home. She waited outside for quite a while, as it was coming from Carson City. Finally, the taxi arrived, and the trip seemed to take forever. As soon as she was safe in her home, she locked her door and cried. I knew it was too good to be true... *I am an Indian, not worthy of Claude... Why? Why??*

She wouldn't answer the door when Claude came by several hours later. He pounded on the door asking for her to let him in, but Joann never answered or said a word. She knew what he was going to tell her and she didn't want to hear it. They were not going to get married. She wasn't good enough. Money was more important to him than her. Joann was angry, as she lay on her bed and loved on Mr. Bojanges, *they will be sorry... All of them. The cat knew all along he was a loser.*

+++

Claude and his drunken Father got into a fight, and he took a belt to Claude for impregnating an Indian squaw. Finally, his mother broke up the incident, wrapping and cleaning Claude's cuts. Claude got away as soon as he could. He loved Joann, but with a baby coming. He was torn, *what do I do?* He knew in reality that he needed his parent's assistance to get through college. Maybe he and Joann could figure something out to do.

+++

Soon as he got back to Carson, he went to Joann's apartment and beat on the door until his knuckles bled. He knew she was home, but wouldn't answer. Not that he could blame her. Claude understood, she was upset. But damn it wasn't his fault! He left, downtrodden and got drunk. *Maybe its best, it ends this way. I don't need a kid right now.*

Chapter Ten

It was October 10, 1962, when baby Brian was born. He was perfect. A beautiful, happy baby boy. Joann was so proud. She would raise her son by herself with the help of Alma, and she would get her revenge someday on Claude and his family. She had plenty of time.

+++

The person Joann had trusted had let her down, just like her parents. She hadn't heard from Claude after that terrible Sunday. He never came to visit or called. Thank goodness she had Alma to assist her through the nine months. There were some scary times. Joann worried if she would be a good parent. Could she handle this? All the typical concerns a parent goes through since she was on her own. Thank goodness for the loving help of Alma. Alma was so excited about being a grandmother. Joann found out she was made of strong stuff. She was quite worthy and would be a great parent because she loved this baby more than anything.

+++

Joann traded in the Chevy for a four-door dark blue 1956 Ford Taurus. She decided to move into a two bedroom duplex, which she rented from Claude's cousin, Jacob Leigh. He was about the same age as Claude. Jacob liked Joann, and she thought *this may come in handy someday.* A type of friendship developed between Joann and Jacob when he came to collect the rent. He would come and visit and have a few beers while Joann drank a Pepsi. It was handy for Joann as she would hear about Claude and what was going on in his life. She found out that Claude had gotten married and just had a daughter. Jacob didn't know that Claude was Brian's father. The only person who knew was Alma.

+++

Brian was a joy. Joann was blessed that Alma, who at sixty-two had retired from the school to babysit while Joann was at work. Alma loved to be referred to as grandmother Alma. Joann told people she worked with, that Brian's Dad had died in the Vietnam War. She didn't want people to see Brian in a bad light as a child with no father.

The first few years were hard to handle, but between her and Alma they did it, and it made Joann stronger, and the anger faded from the surface a little. Joann loved Brian with all her heart, and she knew she would never let anything ever happen to him. Nothing or nobody would ever take her child from her. He would never have to go to an Indian school. Mr. Bojangles even took to the boy. Life was on the right track.

+++

Joann couldn't believe how fast time passed. Over the years, when Jacob came to collect the rent, he would play with the boy. When Brian was five, Jacob brought him a baseball mitt, and they went to Mills Park and played ball. Jacob even took Brian fishing, as he seemed genuinely interested in the boy. Joann and Jacob went to the movies a few times, but she was not ready for another man in her life. Her life was full of work and Brian, and she didn't want to complicate it. Claude now had two daughters, yet had never reached out to see his son.

Before she knew it, Brian was six and started going to school. He got into sports. He was a natural like his Dad. Then a sad thing happened, Mr. Bojanges, who was ten got hit by a car. The vet did everything he could, but Joann had to make the decision to have him put down. This just tore her up, as she loved that darn cat. She and Brian sat holding each other crying, petting the cat, as they said their goodbyes to a member of their family. Joann thought I *don't like losing things I love...*

+++

Time has a habit of flying by when life is busy. Joann couldn't believe it was Brian's birthday again. On Saturday, October 10th, they were celebrating his ninth birthday. Joann took him and three friends for pizza. It was an excellent Indian Summer day and seeing it was so pleasant, they decided to go play in Mills Park. Brian was swinging with his buddies, and Joann was sitting at a picnic table watching the kids play when a voice from behind her said, "Hello Joann."

She didn't turn around, she knew the voice, "what do you want?" She snapped.

"Which one is ours?" he asked.

"None is ours," she stated very coldly.

"Come on Joann, let's heal the wound. He is my son,"

"Go to hell asshole. You made your choice, you wanted money over being married to an Indian and your son..."

"That's not fair, I didn't have a choice. Please look at me,"

"Why? I know what you look like. I understand you are married. Go to your wife," growled Joann.

Joann couldn't leave, as she didn't want Claude to see his son. Instead, she stayed sitting with her back to him. It got quiet, but she didn't want to turn around to see. Finally, she heard his voice over by a car. She quickly looked and could see there were two little girls with him, plus a woman sitting in the car. Jacob had told her, that Claude's wife has cancer, and they can't have any more children, and he doesn't have a son... *oh, my...* Joann was so angry, maybe it is time to get even... Even with them all.

+++

Joann never received welfare when Brian was born, and Claude never sent money for Brian's support. So over the years to help make ends meet, Joann baked cakes and cookies for the local bakery. Everyone loved her goodies. She knew that Claude's parents came in once a week to buy her cookies. Of course, they didn't know she was the baker. Could she poison them like she did Mr. Simmons?... No, that would be too easy, and she wanted them to suffer. She would have to be careful with whatever she did as she didn't want to get caught.

Joann found that Claude's Mom, Edith, has her hair done at a local salon... Have to think about that. Joann knew where Claude's parents lived, and she has to consider that... She knew whatever she did, it had to look like an accident. Joann didn't want to kill them, but she wanted them to lose all their money and suffer.

+++

Mother Nature decided to help Joann, as winter came early and furious. Everywhere in the area received feet of snow, instead of inches, as well as high winds, knocking down trees and power lines. Then a Pineapple Express came in and melted all the snow, floods were everywhere, even in Yerington. Jacob told her that Claude parents were using a generator to pump water out of their flooded basement... A light went on. Joann knew how to get even...

+++

The Nevada Appeal had a big article; "**House Fire in Yerington.**" "Anthony and Edith Stone were hospitalized when their house burned down. A faulty generator used to pump water out their basement produced enough carbon monoxide and smoke to affixiate them as they slept. The Fire Marshal indicated the generator was in their kitchen, which shorted out and caused the fire. Both victims are in bad shape from carbon monoxide and smoke poisoning." The report further said they weren't sure the Stone's would make it.

The irony of this was that Joann hadn't done anything to cause the accident, except to wish it. Joann figured it was karma and it couldn't have happened to better people... Anthony died a couple days later, and Edith's mind was short-circuited from the lack of oxygen. The sad part was they never got to know their grandson, Brian, and now they never would. Joann thought, *There is two down. Now I will get the rest in time.*

The funeral for Anthony Stone was at Walton's Funeral Home. Joann snuck into the back of the room unnoticed and sat down. She thought as the SOB laid in the coffin. *It serves him right, can't take your money with you*. During the service that droned on, she looked at the light above the coffin, it was beautiful five-light sconce. He didn't deserve this gracious of a funeral. From what she understood from Jacob, Anthony was a mean drunk, who beat his wife and kids. Guess he figured money made him a nice person. Hate swelled inside her. She left as soon as the service was over, never speaking to a soul.

Chapter Eleven

Jacob and Brian got along well, during the summer they both went fishing. Jacob was teaching Brian how to gold pan. Sometimes, Joann would go along, but most of the time, she let the boys spend time together. Jacob and Joann would go to dinner and take in a movie. Once she observed Claude and his wife, Debbie, at the theater. She looked terrible, Joann understood she had breast cancer and was not beating it. Joann didn't know her and felt no hate for her... only Claude. Claude was now a high school football coach in Reno. Apparently, they lived in Washoe Valley, according to Jacob.

+++

For Brian twelfth birthday, Jacob wanted to take them to Disneyland in Los Angeles. Brian was so excited that Joann couldn't say no. Joann still didn't have a romantic interest in Jacob. He was good-looking, tall and slender with brown eyes that saw into her soul, but the spark wasn't there. *I don't know if I will ever trust a man again...*

They were to spend a week, seeing Disneyland and Universal Studios. Joann had saved up for the trip. Jacob bought the tickets and found a hotel close by. Joann said she would pay for gas and food. They were going to make the trip during school fall break in October. Joann had a birthday party on Brian's birthday, October tenth, with six of his friends. They went for pizza. He got to tell them about his upcoming trip. Everyone was excited. Some of the boys had been there and told Brian what he had to see.

October fifteenth. Joann will never forget. The phone rang, and Joann answered, "Hello."

"Hi, Joann. Please don't hang up," he said with desperation in his voice. "I needed to talk to someone.

"I'm still here, what's the problem?" asked Joann.

"Debbie is in the hospital, they don't expect her to live through the night."

"I'm sorry for her, but what am I supposed to do about it," she said flippantly.

"What am I going to do without her? I have two daughters, nine and eleven to raise, I know you are raising our son with no help from me. How are you doing it?"

Joann wanted to hang up on the selfish SOB. "You put one foot in front of the other and just keep moving," she said coldly as she hung up. The phone rang again, she didn't answer. She couldn't believe he was that selfish. His wife is dying, and he is only worried about himself. *What had she ever seen in him?* The irony of the phone call was she felt nothing, no anger, just relief. It was over, she didn't care what happened to him. *I am worthy, I don't need to seek revenge against him... Karma got him first.*

+++

At the end of October, Brian, Jacob, and Joann were off to California. Joann had never had a real vacation, so she was as excited as Brian. "Disneyland here we come," they chanted on the drive. Jacob was happy to be with the family he wished was his. Maybe this will be the time to tell Joann, how he feels...

Chapter Twelve

Their vacation was terrific, and they all had so much fun, getting up early and going to bed late. They must have ridden every ride. Joann bought a bunch of souvenirs, T-shirts, and postcards. Brian ate all kinds of junk food, shoot, they all did. She never wanted to forget this trip. Joann really enjoyed Jacob. He was so easy to get along with, and he didn't drink much on the journey.

Like all good things, they had to come home, but they had all kinds of stories to tell. Joann couldn't remember being so happy. Brian couldn't wait to go to school wearing his new T-Shirts saying he went to Disneyland. Jacob was pleased with himself for making both of them so happy.

+++

Debbie Stone passed away while they were gone to Disneyland. Joann did think of telling Brian about his half-sisters for about one minute. The past is the past. Brian's dad is dead to her. Claude hadn't tried calling her again. However,

Joann had gotten a new unlisted number before they left on vacation. She didn't want Claude talking to Brian.

+++

Life got back to normal with school and work. With a child, there has always been plenty to do. Work was hectic. Joann had to catch up from the vacation. Nevertheless, she was glad to be working.

Joann was going to dinner with Jacob on Friday night, and Brian was staying over at a friend's house. Joann felt good and thought the vacation was just what she needed. She wasn't angry with anyone or anything. She thought *this must be how regular people feel... happy.*

Joann wanted to look good for her dinner date, so she fussed over what to wear. Finally, she felt she looked good. When Jacob came to pick her up, he admired how she looked and told her. Jacob took her to dinner at the Nugget Steak House. When they had sat down, he said, "Joann have whatever you want on the menu."

"Really? I could have lobster?" she laughed.

"Yep. Tonight is your night", as he ordered a drink.

The evening was great, they laughed about their vacation and enjoyed their great dinner. They both decided on lobster. Finally, Jacob got serious, "Joann, I would like you to marry me. We have fun together, and I love Brian like he was my own. You don't have to answer me now, but please think about it."

Joann looked at him and without thinking, "Yes. Yes, Jacob, I would love to be your wife."

Jacob jumped up and "Yelled I am getting married."

Everyone in the dining room clapped. Joann blushed, but it was a bright, happy blush.

+++

It was decided they would get married February fourteenth, on Valentine's Day, which gave Joann less than two months to get ready. It would be a simple affair at the Court House. Brian would be best man, and Alma would stand up for Joann. Joann made her dress with Alma help. She also baked her own wedding cake for the small reception at her house. All the plans were set.

+++

Joann and Jacob went to the Court House to get their marriage license since the wedding was next Saturday. Judge Jones would marry them at noon. Now just the wait, seven days seemed like forever. Brian called Jacob, Dad. He was thrilled to have a man in his life.

Finally, the day came, and Joann had to pinch herself. Jacobs's parents really liked her. However, they were a little disappointed that they didn't get married in a chapel. Brian said, "They could get married later in the church." Joann was beside herself, she was worthy of a good man's love. They planned their honeymoon going to Las Vegas. Brian was staying with Alma for the three days. Then, they would come home, and all three of them would go to Ely and see the Leman Caves and Great Basin Park, if possible since it was still winter.

Joann kept saying to herself over and over, *Joann Leigh, Mrs. Joann Leigh... I am Mrs. Joann Leigh.* Jacob and Brian were pretty happy too. The reception went well, Mr. John Leigh, Jacob's dad, had too much to drink and made a pass at Joann. Saying, "If my son doesn't make you happy, I will." Joann didn't respond and blamed it on the booze, little did she know. She thought *nothing was going to ruin this day... not even a drunken father-in-law.*

The time came for them to say their farewells and depart for Vegas. They were staying in Tonopah tonight and would go to Vegas tomorrow. Mr. & Mrs. Jacob Leigh. Joann was finally somebody...

The three days in Vegas were a whirlwind, taking in shows, and Joann got to see Elvis Presley perform. Jacob saved that as a super surprise, she thought she had died from happiness. Jacob, got drunk one night, but that was okay, they were in Vegas. Joann thought this is what ordinary people do, enjoy life and I never want it to end.

When they arrived home, the three of them went to Ely to go to the Great Basin Park. On the road to Ely, there wasn't much traffic, and you might see a car every ten miles after Fallon. This part of the trip was boring, but they talked and sang made up songs. There were no cattle, in fact, nothing to see but high desert. That's why Highway 50 is called the "The Loneliest Road in America." Joann and Brian loved the trip, seeing a part of the state they had never seen before.

When they arrived at the Park, they looked around the gift shop and bought some postcards of the Park and the Lehmans Caves. In the summer you can hike to Wheeler's Peak, one of the highest peaks in Nevada. The tour of the Lehman Caves started at 1:30 p.m. with a guide. Joann and Brian had never been in real caves. In fact, any caves. They hiked down a narrow tunnel to a large cavern, and it was overwhelming. The guide explained that the Lehman Caves consisted of beautiful marble ornately decorated with stalactites, stalagmites, helictites, flowstone, popcorn, and over 300 rare shield formations all with different colors.

The weather in February was cold, but no snow. Jacob took them to a Basque restaurant. The food had lots of garlic, but it was great. He drank a little too much, so Joann drove back to the room. The next day they headed back home, knowing the vacation was over. They would have to journey back to the real world, whether they wanted to or not. But they had a new life ahead of them as a family.

Chapter Thirteen

Even when they got home, they had a few days off, so the honeymoon period continued. Their honeymoon had been so much fun. The more she was around Jacob; the more she learned to love him. She did, however, wish he wouldn't drink so much. Neither one of them wanted this time to end. Nevertheless, life goes on, and they had to get back to a normal life. Brian had to go to school and Joann and Jacob back to work.

It was decided that they would move into Jacobs house since it was bigger than her apartment. Also, the extra income from renting her apartment would help. It didn't take long for them to settle into a routine.

+++

As in any life, you have the good with the bad. Over the next couple of years, Joann tried to get pregnant, but it didn't happen. After several tests, it seems, Jacob couldn't have children. His sperm count was too low. The doctor told him alcohol did affect it.

"It's okay if you want, we could adopt?" stated Joann.

"No! No adoption, we have Brian, that's enough," as he finished his fourth beer.

"We are both getting older, do you really think we should start a family?" asked Joann with a smile.

"It's a moot question... I can't father children," he snarled as he slammed the beer can on the table.

Joann let the subject drop. The apartment had been vacant again, and they had rented it to a young couple. Joann started talking about the new renters, "Mr. and Mrs. Brown seems nice. I think they are going to work out fine. What do you think?"

"Yeah. Yeah, they will be okay," as he staggered into the front room. Joann though *I am happy Brian wasn't home for this scene.*

+++

Over time, things didn't get better, Joann thought *it had to be me. He's drunk every night and passes out on the couch. What am I going to do? Do I leave?* She had no one to talk to about this problem, not even Alma. She thought *I deserved better than this.*

+++

Jacob didn't want to do anything with her or Brian, just drink. Joann had planned a birthday party for Brian, as he was going to be fifteen. They had decided on a pizza party/sleepover. Brian had asked several of his best friends to spend the night. They all had their sleeping bags in the front room, watching Creature Feature on the TV when Jacob staggered into the front room in his shorts. He proceeded to pass out on the couch. Brian's friends laughed.

Brian was so embarrassed. Joann ran into the room and tried to get Jacob to bed. After a struggle, put a blanket on him and let him sleep it off on the couch. She made popcorn for the kids, and everything went on as normal, but Joann was furious. Brian never invited friends over again.

+++

Joann tried talking to Jacob about his drinking, and he would tell her to go to hell and leave him alone. "You don't understand what I am going through," he shouted at her.

"And you don't understand what you are doing to this family," she shouted back. Jacob just looked at her and stormed out the door.

+++

Once, his folks came by in the evening and observed their son's drunkenness. His Mother, Iris, was rocking him telling him all will be okay. "Leave me alone, Mother," he slurred.

Iris came into the kitchen with her hands on her hips, "Well Injun, what have you done to my son?"

Joann looked at Iris in disbelief standing there with her hands on her hips. "What did you call me?"

"Injun, you heard me," Iris snarled.

Joann just looked at her, "get out of my house, both of you... now, before this Injun goes on the warpath," snapped Joann.

"Don't speak to my wife in that tone," growled John.

"Get out now!! Both of you!" They grabbed their coats and headed for the door. Iris said, "Jacob come with us."

He just looked at her and passed out. Iris screamed, "You have drugged him," she yelled at Joann, "John help me get him out of this house before she kills him." The two picked Jacob up and led him out the door. Joann was so upset, she was shaking, and her gut churned. *It's always my fault because I am an Indian... You want to see who fault it is, you haven't seen anything yet!!*

Chapter Fourteen

Joann told Brian that Jacob wasn't doing well and would be staying with his parents for a while. He was upset, and said, "Jacob doesn't like me anymore."

"No, he just has a problem he needs to work through. Therefore, we'll be moving. I am sorry Brian.

"It is okay, Mom, we have been alone before, we can handle this." Joann gave him a big hug, "Such a big boy, I love you so much."

"I love you too Mom; I'll take care of us."

+++

She found a two-bedroom apartment she could afford, and within two days, they had moved out. Joann was so glad she had some money saved to assist with the move. She still hadn't heard from Jacob.

+++

A week or better had gone by, no word from Jacob. Joann came out of her office to go for lunch and waiting in the parking lot was Jacob. She stopped, and he came over, looking like hell. "Hi Joann, can we go somewhere to talk?"

"There is nothing to talk about Jacob, remember I'm an Injun...," snapped Joann

He looked at her with a sad face, "I never called you that," explained Jacob.

"No you didn't, but your sweet Mom did, and you never defended me," responded Joann.

"I'm so sorry; you know I never saw you like that. I love you," replied Jacob.

"Yeah, I notice how much you love me these past months," growled Joann.

"I'm sorry, I'll try to be better, please come home."

"No. I do not trust you or your family. Brian and I will be okay. Thanks for asking about him..."

"I'm not thinking straight. How is he doing? I'm sorry; I have lost my job because I have to have back surgery." He said with his mouth quivering.

"I'm sorry for your bad luck... Karma is a bitch." Joann started to walk to her car.

"Please come home, Joann, I need you." He stood there as she got into her car and drove off.

Joann went to the closest restaurant and ordered a salad. She wasn't hungry, but she had to eat. I have to think this out. *I must come up with a plan to get even... this crap that occurred cannot be forgiven. No one hurts my son's feelings. We are more worthy than any of them...* After a couple of weeks, she had it figured out. The plan will now be put in place. *The patience of a snake.*

+++

Several weeks passed before she called Jacob and invited him to dinner. He was still staying at his parent's house. Jacob jumped at the invitation and showed up with flowers and a new baseball mitt for Brian.

The dinner was cordial, everyone acted like it was old times, and nothing terrible had occurred. "When are you to have your surgery?" Joann asked.

"In two weeks. I'll be laid up for six weeks, and if all goes well will get my job back," responded Jacob.

"What are you having done?" Joann inquired.

"They are replacing two discs in my lower back. I fell out of a loader from slipping on the ice on a step."

"Ouch."

"A little more than an ouch, I'm on heavy duty pain pills."

"Awww so you can't drink?"

"Not for now," then he saw her face. "However, I will probably quit."

81

"Yeah, sure."

The rest of the evening went slow, and Joann couldn't wait for him to leave. She found out what she wanted to know, and nothing had changed. He would go back to drinking as soon as he was well. *What is wrong with me, why do I pick losers... well, I gave him his chance, now the plan goes into play.*

+++

Joann didn't file for divorce. She wasn't going to let him off the hook that easy. Jacob kept hoping they would resolve everything, especially when she went to the hospital with him. He really did love her, but he knew a lot of damage had been done. His parents were at the hospital too. Joann though this will be interesting. They sat on opposite sides of the waiting room, not talking. Iris wouldn't even look at her. John caught her eye and smiled. *Asshole* thought Joann.

The tension built in the waiting room as several hours passed. Finally, Joann went to the cafeteria for something to drink and get away from his parents. She was afraid she would throw something at them. Joann no sooner got back to the waiting room than the Doctor came out and called for her. He told her all was fine and Jacob would be in recovery for a couple of hours, then she could visit. She thanked him and walked out of the waiting room, looking back to see his parents jumping up to grab the doctor, but he had gone back through the doors. Joann smiled to herself.

Several hours later Joann and Brian went to see Jacob, who was still groggy but glad to see them. Brian brought him a get well card. His parents were not there, they had come and gone. After about twenty minutes, Joann and Brian left. Jacob was going to be okay, the operation was a success.

Chapter Fifteen

Jacob got his old job back, and things were almost normal. He had moved back to his house and kept asking Joann to move home. They went to dinner every week, Joann was taking things slow, let him suffer.

Several months later, Joann did move back into Jacobs house. Things seemed okay on the surface, Jacob drinking had slowed down, but she was still scheming. Brian got his learner's permit, and Joann was teaching him to drive.

Jacob came home one day with a big smile on his face, "Brian, please come outside with me."

Brian was hesitant, "Why?"

"I have something for you."

Everyone went outside to see what was going on and there in the driveway was a 1954 pickup. " I bought this for you, You and I can work on it, but it's yours."

Brian looked at Jacob amazed, "Thank you for the truck. You didn't have to."

"I know, but I wanted to. You are getting to be a grown boy and need a truck for fishing and hunting," replied Jacob. With that, the two took the truck for a drive. Brian was beaming. Joann almost cried, but kept quiet, then she thought, *maybe Jacob is changing.*

By the time they came back, Joann had dinner on the table. First thing Jacob did before he sat down, was grab a beer. By the time dinner was done, Jacob had drunk three more beers. Joann thought *nothing had changed. But this time I will put it to good use.*

Jacob passed out on the couch that night. It was the first time in a while, and Joann just put a blanket on him and left him there. After that, it became a nightly ritual.

+++

Life did change in the Leigh household. Joann encouraged Jacob to drink, always made sure there was a cold beer in the frig. She and Brian did things without Jacob, or Brian was with his friends. Joann was hoping Jacob would drink himself to death. She didn't care anymore. She had pride. Apparently, white men don't, but he was her cross to bear.

+++

On Saturday, Brian was gone to the Lake with his friends and Jacob was working overtime, John came by. Joann met him at the door and said, "Jacob is not here."

"I know, I came to see you," he slurred.

Joann could tell he had been drinking. Like Father like son. She wouldn't let him in as she stood in the doorway, "Why do you want to see me?" she asked, her heart racing.

He pushed her out of the way, "To have my way with you, Injun."

"Get out. Get out now," Joann screamed.

With that, he slapped her hard enough to knock her to the floor and jumped on top of her, tearing at her clothes as he tried to rape her. The skin on Joann arms pimpled and her throat went dry, *not again*, terror welled in her throat. *Why me?* Joann was looking to find something to hit him with, when all of a sudden he rolled off grabbing his chest, panting. She squirmed out of his grip and stood over him. He was howling in pain, "call an ambulance, I'm having a heart attack."

Joann just stood there. "Damn it Injun call the paramedics." Sweat was pouring out of him, and his face was gray. Joann never moved. She thought, *karma is a bitch for the way you have treated me, I am worthy.* After a few minutes of watching him, he passed out. Joann walked into the bathroom and straightened herself up before walking back to the front room. John was still; she felt him, and there was a light pulse.

She straightened the front room, and then called the ambulance. "Please come quickly, my father-in-law is having, I think a heart attack." She said in a panic-stricken voice. And proceeded to give her address. It took them about five minutes to get there.

They came rushing in with their equipment and started working on John but to no avail. "I am sorry, but he's gone," said one of the medics. Joann started to cry, which was hard for her because she wanted to laugh. She thought, *serves you right, you SOB. Joann's stomach had soured, but she felt no remorse.*

When Jacob got home, he asked her, "Why did he come to the house? "

"To see you," she replied.

"Funny, he knew I was working."

"Well, it is a good thing he did, or he could have died driving a car."

"Good point," and Jacob left it at that.

The house was a zoo. When she called Jacob to come home, the cops came which is normal when there's death, as well as the coroner. Jacob called his Mom, and they took the body to Waltons. After an hour or so, things quieted down. Joann thought, *well, that wasn't planned, but what the heck, one down, two to go...*

Chapter Sixteen

Even though John was cremated, they had a full Catholic funeral that lasted for over an hour. Joann couldn't wait to leave. Iris leaned on Jacob and his other brother Ray. Joann and Brian sat back away from her. The reception after the funeral would be held at Iris's house. Joann begged away, saying she had a terrible headache. Brian drove her home. Jacob was concerned for Joann, but stayed, as he should, with his family. No one else in the family missed them.

Brian went to visit friends once he got his Mom home. He really didn't care for his step-grandfather, but he never told his Mom, that John said hateful things about her. He asked Brian one time how it felt to be a half-breed? Brian was hurt, but came back with, "great I am the best of two worlds." That shut John up. Brian wasn't crazy about Iris, but she was Jacob's Mom, so he showed her respect.

Joann really did have a terrible headache, as she lay on the bed, she thought, *how did my life get here? I have been directly involved with the death of three people, wish death on a couple and planning on killing a couple more. What kind of monster have I become?* Then her mind would argue, *you are not a monster. Your life was stolen, and people don't appreciate you. They are getting what they deserve. You are somebody!!* Finally, sleep took over while she tossed and turned.

+++

Jacob didn't come home until the next morning, and he was drunk, "Ray and I stayed up all night talking about Dad. Sorry. I should have called."

"Not a problem, I was asleep most of the time... with this darn headache."

"How are you feeling?" As he sat on the bed next to her.

"Better, it's let up for now. Just too much stress lately. Your Dad dying here and all."

"Well, it's not a surprise, as he has had a bad heart for years. But I am surprised he died here. Still, can't figure out why he came by?"

"To see you," as she turned away from him.

"But he knew where I was, just doesn't make sense," stated Jacob.

"I don't know what to tell you. Please, I don't want to talk about it anymore, my headache is starting to come back," complained Joann.

"Sorry Hon," as he lay down on the bed. In a matter of minutes, he was snoring away.

Joann got up from the bed, walked to the bathroom, where she promptly threw up. *I don't know if I can keep this up.*

+++

In February, Joann got a call from Alma, she wasn't feeling well. Joann drove right over to find Alma in bed, looking like a ghost. "Oh, my gosh, what is going on?"

"I don't know, but I just don't feel good," responded Alma.

"Well, I am taking you to the hospital, right now. Let's get up."

Alma struggled to get out of bed, and between the two they couldn't get her out of bed. Joann called 911. "I need an ambulance" and gave them Alma's address.

It seemed like hours, but only a few minutes went by when the medics arrived, bringing in the gurney and their equipment. They started checking Alma vitals when she passed out. Quickly placing her on the stretcher, they drove to the hospital with Joann following them. Joann thought *I can't lose Alma, she is like my Mother. She and Brian are the only people I truly love, I don't want her to die...*

At Carson Tahoe hospital, the nurses were running all over, putting an IV in and taking blood work, a Technician hooked Alma to an EKG machine. Joann sat out of the way and watched. Joann did something she had never done, she prayed to her Creator not to let Alma die. *Please allow her to live, I will change, I will try. Please, I need her in my life.*

Alma was starting to come around, looking dazed. Joann ran over to her and grabbed her hand. "Everything is going to be okay, Alma."

"Thank you, nurse," murmured Alma.

Joann started to cry. Alma didn't know who she was. Joann asked the nurse, "What is going on?"

"You will have to talk to the Doctor, sorry."

Joann sat back down again out of the way and watch what was going on. Nurses, technicians, and doctors came and went, all working on Alma. Alma was still passed out or sleeping, but her coloring was a little better, and it wasn't so gray. Joann had never been so scared. *I can't lose this woman. She is the only person besides Brian that loves me. Damn, Joann, quit thinking about yourself...*

The next forty-eight hours were pure hell. Thank goodness Alma pulled through this time. She was on the verge of a stroke, but little damage was done, as they had gotten her to the hospital in time. The Doctor told Joann to go home and get some rest as the worse was over.

The following morning Joann came to visit, and Alma was sitting up in bed reading the paper, she looks like her usual self, Joann was so relieved. She ran over to the bed and gave her a big hug. "I'm so glad to see you are feeling better. I was so worried I would lose you."

"Fit as a fiddle, and the world would be better if they fed you decent food in here," chimed Alma. Joann laughed.

"What did the Doctor say about what is going on?" asked Joann.

"I have to take it easy, he says, the old ticker is slowing down, but I will be fine. You know you can't kill a stubborn Irishwoman," smiled Alma.

"Well, I know one thing, you're moving in with me, so I can take care of you, proper diet, etc. No arguments you hear?" stated Joann.

Alma looked at her with a tear in her eye, "You sure you want an old lady around?"

"More than anything in the world," as she gave Alma a big hug. Joann thought *I am going to turn my life around, and it starts now with saving Alma's.*

Chapter Seventeen

Several days later Alma moved into the guest room. Joann forwarned Jacob to be on his best behavior or else. She left only three beers in the refrig. Time to wean him. Life was going to change for them all.

Things went okay for a week or so, then Jacob started coming home late and going straight to bed, saying he had visited his Mom or whatever. Joann knew he was drinking somewhere, and Brian knew it too. Days continued into weeks, and basically, they hardly saw him. He hadn't had dinner with them for weeks. One morning Alma asked, "Is Jacob upset because I am here?"

"No. Alma, Jacob is a drunk, and I told him he couldn't drink around you, so he drinks elsewhere. That simple." The look on Joann's face was pure disgust and hate. "I'm used to people blaming me for everything because I'm an Indian. If he really loved me, he would try to make this relationship work, but he never has. Once he found out he couldn't have children..." she paused "I just don't give a damn anymore."

"I'm so sorry Joann, I didn't know. You poor child."

Joann saw the tears in Alma's eyes, "I'm sorry I shouldn't have upset you with my problems. We need to keep you well; you and Brian are all I have."

Alma patted her hand, "Jacob loves you too, he just doesn't know how to show it."

"There are times when I just wish he would die and end all this misery..." whispered Joann. "I hate my life, except for you and Brian. My life has never been fair, plus I never made the right choices when I had the chance... something is missing in me."

Ama looked at her and shook her head. "Nothing missing in you. Joann, let me tell you a story. My grandparents migrated to America from Ireland because of the potato famine in the 1800s. Basically, it was a genocide of the Irish by the English. I grew up in a house that hated Catholics, and my family was poor with little education. My Dad died, leaving my sickly mother with five children. So at the early age of nine, I was hired out, basically as an indentured slave to a wealthy family named Normandy also with five children, whose father, Johnathan liked to use a bullwhip." Alma pulled up her blouse and showed Joann her scars on her back.

Joann stared in shock, "You must have hated this man?"

"Worse than that, at the ripe age of twelve, he beat and raped me, not once but several times. So, over time, I killed him with my cooking. Thank goodness I never got caught, sort of like what you did when you killed Mr. Simmons."

A shocked look came over Joann's face, "You knew?"

"Sure, I'd done the same thing." They both hugged each other. "Life wasn't fair to either of us. But we survived."

"What happen to you?" asked Joann.

"The man's wife, Mary, was a kind woman, but very timid, but was pleased to be rid of him. However, she didn't know I killed him. She may have suspected, but never said anything to anyone. She treated me as one of her own children and send me to school. I was able to get a job and go to college and become a teacher. Well, you know the rest of the story."

"Did life get better for you, being Irish and all?" Question Joann.

"Well, that's the funny part, I had been taught to hate Catholics, and the Normandy's were Catholic. I tried to hate Mary and her children, I did hurt one of them, but they were good to me, she even forgave me when I hurt Derek... I broke his arm."

"I can't believe you would hurt anyone, you are so kind," stated Joann.

"I wasn't always, I was full of hate. Nevertheless, Mary never gave up on me. It took years, and I imagine there were times she wanted to throw me out with the bath water. I would catch her praying for me."

"She was there like you have been here for me," Joann put her face in her hands and cried like a baby.

Alma stood up and hugged her, "All is going to be okay, you will see."

"I have hurt so many people. No. That is not true. I only hurt the people who hurt me," Joann said defiantly.

"Oh. We do have some work to do, don't we?" sighed Alma.

+++

As time passed, Alma got stronger. She had a mission. Joann was true to her word. She tried to be kind, and get Jacob to see a doctor for his drinking. He would come home now, eat dinner and pass out on the couch. This was pretty much the nightly event. This lasted for about a month, then he started not coming home, he didn't want to change.

Brian was going to graduate from high school and was planning on going to college. He had received a scholarship to go to Idaho University. He wanted to be an engineer. Joann tried to talk him into going to UNR as they have a great engineering school. But the truth of the matter, Brian wanted to get away from Jacob, who was a full fledge drunk. He couldn't understand why his Mother put up with him being drunk all the time. They had fought about it a few times, and Joann replied, "I married him for better or worse."

The sad part was Jacob used to be fun, and Brian missed that Jacob. When Jacob was sober, it could still be fun. But they didn't go fishing or hunting anymore, all Jacob wanted to do was drink. Brian couldn't wait to leave home, though he would miss his Mom and Alma.

+++

Alma was like Brian's Grandma, she would be eighty this coming Thursday. He would miss them when he left on Saturday for Idaho. He was leaving early as he had found a job on a ranch for the summer to earn extra money and was sharing an apartment with a friend who got a football scholarship. Plus, he was excited to be on his own, He was now eighteen. The worst part was leaving his Mom, but thank goodness she had Alma to take care of and go places with.

Joann had planned a little party for Brian and Alma to celebrate her birthday and his going away. Alma had been good for Joann, she had mellowed her over the years, her anger and hate was almost gone. She didn't even hate Jacob anymore, she felt sorry for him. He was still a drunk, but it was his choice. The sad part he had missed so much of Brian's life. Jacob may show up for the party and maybe not... Joann had mixed emotions about that. She didn't want Jacob to embarrass Brian in front of his friends, though most of them knew about Jacob.

The party was a great success. Jacob didn't come, and Joann hadn't seen him in several days. He didn't come to see Brian leave. Joann looked at her son, he had grown into a handsome young man, and he stood six feet tall with his dad's good-looking features, wavy brown hair, and her olive complexion and dark piercing eyes. She was so proud of him. He never felt the misery she had felt growing up, and for that, she was thankful to her Creator. She loved this boy with all her heart, and for the first time in her life, she felt blessed.

Alma and Joann cried when Brian left, their boy had grown up and left the nest. But they made plans to come and visit him in a few months when school started.

Brian called the next day to say they made the trip okay and he and Jeff were settled into the apartment. Joann was relieved. Things were going well, and a new chapter of life was happening.

+++

About six months later: Around two in the morning she heard knocking on the front door, throwing on a robe, she ran to the door, and there stood a policeman.

"Good evening, are you Joann Leigh?"

"Yes." From the look on his face, she knew something terrible had happened, *Oh my, something happened to Brian...*"What happened?

""Your husband Jacob Leigh is in Carson Tahoe Hospital. He's been in a car accident."

"What is it," yelled Alma.

"It's Jacob, he has been in a car accident," yelled Joann.

"Oh, my God," cried Alma as she came running out of her bedroom.

"How bad Officer?" Asked Joann.

""Bad."

Joann ran to the bedroom to get dressed, while Alma talked to the Officer. Within five minutes Joann was dressed and ready to go. "I will follow you, Officer." They left for the hospital. "I'll call you Alma."

Joann pulled into the emergency and ran inside, asking for her husband. The nurse very casually said "room 8B." Joann started to go, "You can't go in" growled the nurse, "have a seat in the waiting room, we'll call you."

"What?" and the Nurse just glared at her. Joann sat down and grabbed a magazine, but couldn't concentrate on reading. Twenty minutes must have passed by, seem like twenty hours. Finally, a Doctor came out. "Are you Mrs. Leigh?"

"Yes, Sir."

"You can come back now, we have him stable, but it is not good."

"What has happened?

"He was in a car wreck."

Joann *thought no shit,* "but what is wrong with him?"

"It is more like what isn't wrong?"

I am going to kill this guy... so help me... They entered Jacobs's room. He had tubes going everywhere. "He is currently in a coma," replied the Dr.

Joann thought *I remember when I used to pray he would die, but do I want him to now?... I don't know.* She sat in the chair and looked at all the equipment and the man in bed who was her husband basically in name only for the last few years. Did she care for him anymore?

The Dr, said, "we are not sure if he is brain dead, we will know more in twenty-four hours, if he is, you can pull the plug."

Now was her chance to get even... *Did she still want revenge*

Chapter Eighteen

Brian came home for the funeral, it was a Catholic funeral. Not many people came. Joann sat with Brian and Alma. Jacob's family sat together, Joann no longer had to be a family with them anymore. She wanted nothing to do with them, as they would always see her as an Indian. All the confidence Joann had built, was torn down by his family. At the funeral Claude, his new wife, grown daughters and his young son showed up, sitting with Jacob's family. Brian asked who they were, Alma stepped in and said we will talk about it at home. Claude never acknowledged Brian nor did Joann respond to him. Joann felt karma would take care of him, let there be peace.

The other good thing out of all of this was that Jacob died on his own. Joann however, would always wonder, would she have pulled the plug?

+++

Joann couldn't believe how time had flown. During the past years, Joann and Alma had gone to visit Brian in Idaho several times while he was in college. They even traveled to the big city of Las Vegas for Brian's senior Christmas vacation, and they stayed on the strip. Two old broads, well one old broad and one getting there, since Joann was almost fifty. They had a great vacation. Alma had never been there.

They stayed at MGM and visited all the casinos on the strip. Joann hired a scooter for Alma so she could get around and away then went. Alma couldn't believe what she saw, Treasure Island, Volcanos, Pyramid's, riding a boat in a casino. Alma was like she was seventy again. Brian got a kick out of her.

Joann never ever considered getting remarried, even though she had some fine gentlemen chasing after her. Jacob had left her well off, and for that she was thankful. She was thinking of retiring in a few years, as she would have thirty years of state service.

+++

Last October, Alma had her eighty-fifth birthday. In May, Brian graduated from college and moved back home. He obtained a job in Reno with an upcoming Engineering company and was working on his Civil Engineering license through the University of Nevada.

He was looking for an apartment in Reno, but before he found one, as luck would have it, Brian was involved in a car accident on his way to work. It happened on I-80 and Brian was transported to Renown Hospital there in Reno. Joann almost died when she got the call. She left work and drove like a maniac to the hospital, her mind racing with all kinds of terrible thoughts. Was this her Karma for all the things she had done.

Thank goodness, he only received a broken rib from his seat belt. Some idiot came across three lanes and rear-ended Brian as he was trying to get off the freeway. Brian laughed, said, "guessed the guy was late or work."

However, while in the hospital, Brian met the cutest nurse in the ER, it was love at first sight. Brian started dating Nancy Sweetman, all five feet of blond, bubbly, fun. They make the cutest couple, him six feet with dark hair and olive complexions and her, all of five feet, pale complexion with big blue eyes. You couldn't help but notice them, plus they were always smiling and laughing. They enjoyed each other so much.

Joann and Alma just loved her, she fitted right into the family. Being a nurse, Nancy helped in keeping an eye on Alma, who was starting to show her age. Alma now uses a walker and on occasion forgets things. Joann didn't know what she would do when Alma went to meet her Creator.

+++

The next year on Valentine's Day, Brian and Nancy became officially engaged with their wedding planned for the middle of July, at Lake Tahoe. Joann looked forward to that day. They had lots of work to accomplish in five months, all the baking, decorations, bridal shower, and invitations. Nancy's Mom, Martha was also helping so it would be easy. The bridal shower was being handled by Nancy's sister Susie, so it was a family affair. Nancy had bought a beautiful dress at a wedding fair.

Joann was making the wedding cake. A five-tier cake with different flavors, decorated with fresh flowers. Dinner and dancing on the Tahoe Queen, a boat that sails on beautiful Lake Tahoe; it will be such a grand affair. They invited two hundred people to attend. The couple would honeymoon in Hawaii for a week. Joann thought, *before long there might be grandchildren. Maybe...*

+++

Finally, the big day arrived. She and Alma were going together. They had all worked hard on this wedding. The cake was up on the boat, and everything was ready to go. Brian and Nancy were already at the ship with the rest of the family. She and Alma would meet them there.

While getting ready to leave for the wedding, Joann stopped for a moment, looked in the mirror, and couldn't believe she was the same person. Older and wiser, maybe? She really had changed. She had committed sins, yet she learned she was worthy after all, of love and family.

The anger was still there, but less of it. Regrets for her passion and what she had done in the past had faded, as she had made amends with her Creator. As bad as it may sound, she has no regrets for what she had done.

She had lost so much as a child that was her "soul wound." Nevertheless, today as an adult, she has made her own family. Let the healing begin. Joann still has a ways to go, but she is a survivor and a damn proud Indian! She is Tibe!

History of Stewart School

"In 1888, the Nevada Legislature passed a bill that authorized the sale of bonds to purchase land for an Indian boarding school. It was named for Nevada's first U.S. Senator, William Morris Stewart, who also sponsored the national legislation creating this off-reservation boarding school (the only one in Nevada) for American Indian children. The Institute itself was the only Federal Indian school set up by an act of the State Legislature. Once purchased, the land was conveyed to the Bureau of Indian Affairs, who established the boarding school to train and educate Indian children with the ultimate goal of assimilation. Children from Nevada and throughout the West were forced to attend the Stewart Institute up to secondary school age. Students came from many tribes, including the Nevada-based Washoe and Paiute tribes, as well as Hopi, Apache, Pima, Mohave, Walapai, Ute, Pipage, Cocopah and Tewa.

The campus opened December 17, 1890, with a capacity for 100 students that included a Victorian-style wood framed dormitory and schoolhouse. As enrollment increased, new buildings included shops for training, a hospital, and a recreation room was added. A Virginia and Truckee Railroad stop was established in 1906 to deliver supplies and facilitate transporting students to and from the school until 1950.

By 1919, 400 students attended the school. Students learned stone masonry from their teachers, which included Hopi stonemasons and they constructed over sixty native stone buildings. The stones came from the Abe Curry's pit. By the end of the Stewart Indian School era, the complex consisted of eighty-three buildings on two hundred and forty acres of landscaped campus. The State of Nevada has since reacquired the land, and there is now the Stewart Indian School Museum, which is open to the public." (Stewart Indian School History)

Today, the school is listed on the National Register of Historic Places, and the Stweart Indian School Cultural Center is located in the former Administration Building. The museum presents memorabilia that reflect the history of the school.

When the school was open, the classes included reading, writing, and arithmetic. However, they mainly focused on vocational training for the various trades, agriculture, and the service industry. Boy's classes offered, included ranching and farming, mechanics, woodworking, painting, and carpentry and sports. The girl's courses offered were in clerical, baking, cooking, sewing, laundry, and practical nursing. The students' products supplied many of the school's basic needs. "Vocational training remained the school's principal focus until a shift to academics occurred in the late 1960s." (Stewart Indian School History)

The primary purpose of the school; was to teach necessary trades and to assimilate young American Indians into mainstream American culture. In other words, they must learn to be civilized. Assimilation policies such as the prohibition of speaking native languages and practicing native customs anguished both students and their parents. Also, the taking of children from the family broke traditional bonds...Thus the "Soul Wounds."

Finally, the Federal policy toward American Indians radically changed due to the Indian Reorganization Act of 1934. Nevertheless, it took years for it to be put in place.

In later years, the Stewart Indian School encouraged students to speak their native languages and promoted classes in indigenous cultures. Nevertheless, the damage to many Native American traditions had already occurred.

In 1980, the Stewart Indian School closed its doors because of federal budget cuts and earthquake safety issues with the masonry buildings. Nevertheless, many Indian schools still exist today, in other States.

Thank you for reading "Not Worthy, Story of Revenge." If you enjoyed it, please subscribe to my mailing list to hear about future books! jaycrowleybooks@gmail.com

Made in the USA
Middletown, DE
23 March 2019